THE Poppy COLLECTOR

Remembrance Anthology

COLIN DENNIS

The Poppy Collector
Poem Anthology

First published in 2021
www.colindennisbooks.com
Published by Sprocket and Tubs

For Lottie
and
Matthew

Contents

The Jolley Roger Crew

Here's to the crew that nobody knew
That flew the Jolley Roger
Stealthy-still beneath the sea
Brave, dark aquatic lodger

There to sweat on nerves of steel
No comfort, joy, or leisure
Sneak around the ocean floor
Chase down their skulking treasure

No eyes to see, nor sound to make
Be sure they're no one's fodder
So, here's to you, that noble crew
That flew the Jolley Roger

Brave Little Soldier

It wasn't what I'd hoped for
The day you flew home to me
Grim soldiers marching slowly
No tasty afternoon tea

A single trumpet blowing
No pomp, or marching band
Emotions that came flowing
I didn't understand

Holding hands beside the runway
My sister, mum, and me
They said he's on the airplane
But you didn't come to be

Standing straight I held my breath
Not flinch, nor fuss, for me
Your bravest little soldier
I know that I must be

Buckle Up!

Buckle up fey ne'er-do-wells
For now's, the time for battle
Unfurl and show your colours true
In fear your sabres rattle

Stand firm beneath the banner fair
Form squares to hide behind
Taste the blood upon your lips
Thin redcoats, three-deep lined

The roll call bugle answered
Forgotten questions why
Go ask your fallen comrades
Brave souls that came to die

Captain Tom

Marching off to a different beat
My final battle fought
The 'Last Post' now is calling me
For peace that we all sought

Queen's shilling, I had taken
Young fist that grasped the coin
Across the empty parade ground
To comrades now I join

If you should ever pass my way
May your features never harden
For I gave you all my fond farewell
From around my own back garden

Dogs Dinner

I hear the black hound howling
I turn to hide away
I feel its breath come stalking
I am it's wounded prey

Dark shadow on the doormat
Dull gnawing in my head
The sound of the hunted falling
That moment full of dread

I did not heed the scratching
Nor seek its sullen tone
And yet I know I feed it
So tired down to the bone

I fear the black hound calling
Its strength I cannot fight
No sword nor shield or armour
Can slay this darkened Knight

Reaching out for substance
Like swimming for the shore
I long to see it vanquished
To challenge me no more

Down among the Poppies

Laying there below us
Forgotten voices cry
Laid among the poppies
And so, the years go by

A swaying crimson blanket
Crocheted by the storm
Arm in arm together
Forever keep them warm

The seed of youth now taken
On broken foreign fields
Down among the poppies
Their swords to never wield

Karmalite

Armed only with my karmalite
I aim to do no wrong
Justice has been served by me
Now I'm twice as strong

Shuffling with my karmalite
I aim to walk the night
On echoed street my footsteps fall
'Till darkness turns to light

Heavy is my karmalite
I aim to serve you well
A hostage will I be no more
At peace, my story tell

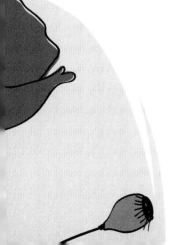

Lonely

Do you know what lonely is
Said the man without a vest
Let me then explain to you
So, you can tell the rest

Lonely's not a choice that's made
To somewhere dark and hollow
A Grimm-like trail of breadcrumbs
Where cold and hunger follow

Lonely isn't a meal for one
Or a café warm inside
Lonely is a soul that's lost
With nowhere left to hide

Remember Me

How shall you remember me
As the bugle call is played
To pass among the headstones
Solemn still while on parade

How shall you remember me
While the poppy flowers grow
Will you rest your hand upon me
Now that peace is all I know

How shall you remember me
Red sun begins to set
Upon the grass I feel your steps
Lost friendship halfway met

Songs we sang together shared
Our time was meant to be
Of freedom forever grateful
I hope you'll remember me

Sail Away

Why go when all you have is here
Why sail the world around
Do you search for some lost soul
No feet on solid ground

Missing plays and childhood ways
Sticking plasters on my knee
The hidden smile that cuts my face
For all the world to see

I wonder where you lay your head
Some far-forgotten land
But you're not here to show and tell
Nor build castles in the sand

Postcards sent from eastern shores
Cold Christmas comes and goes
How long till we are yours again
For heaven only knows

Some days

I taste the splash of puddles
Another rainy day
I hear the sound of silence
The noise that clouds my way

Empty café on the corner
I sip, but I can't stay
The bitter taste of coffee
And so, begins the day

Washed upon the sidewalk
Soft dreams my head to lay
My step forever quickens
Long days that drift away

The needle on the record
Sad song forever plays
I look up to the ceiling
And hope for better days

Known Only

It's not the one we gave you
The name they took away
Come and gone forever
Young life no longer play

No name tag on the collar
Nor etched upon your cross
Broken backs to carry
Shoulder this sad loss

Knowing that you lay there
In some forgotten field
Soldiers of the morning
Fight and never yield

Cabinet Members

Her cabinet full of memories
Polished every day
With soporific camphor
No dust to wipe

She's picking up the pieces
Each a love untold
With smiling heavy burden
Bright eyes grow weary old

Placed minute precision
Like soldiers on parade
Her cabinet full of memories
A life she'd never trade

Some Mother's Son

Lying still, he wanders home
Black streets and solemn skies
Mothers call as darkness falls
Forgotten sons, their fallen prize

Scudding clouds like fever pass
Soothing clean his blooded brow
Sacrificed for king and country
Bury deep this sacred cow

Etched on bone-white crosses
Artisan shall carve his name
Known only unto someone's God
Never cried with endless shame

The Poppy Collector

An usherette from cinema past
Serene her chosen words
Curt nod to please and thank you
Sad smile reminds the world

Red button for her grey coat
Her poppy pride of place
Perennial bloom returning
No onerous task to face

Holding out her damp tray
The penny drops in loud
On high street busy corner
Heavy burden carried proud

Stainless pin that punctures
Smeared blood upon your finger
Suffering bleak November rain
The poppy collector lingers

The Melancholic Warrior

Across the years we've fallen
Bled dry on field and sea
Cannon spews out bitter smoke
Flames once beckoned me

Our shoulders pressed together
We huddled from the storm
Dashed in Hell's formation
Flesh so easy torn

Medals scrubbed and polished
Broken heroes on parade
Lost comrades line the rollcall
Freedom's cost repaid

Placebo

Is there a single pill to take
Sweet sugar cut my lip
Heading down the rabbit hole
Shooting from the hip

Putting on the kettle
Mash a pot of tea
Swallow all the bitterness
Raw freedom guaranteed

Calling up my old friends
But everyone is out
I take the pill to comfort
Inside I scream and shout

Paranoia

A thousand voices fill my head
Not one of them a friend
Mistrust sparks the conflict
Wrong messages they send

Strangers passing comment
Pale oddity am I
Ever grow suspicious
Now everyone's a spy

Curling out my barbed wire
Hanging on a thread
Cold War fever threatens
Blind paranoia bred

Conspiracy Theory

The world conspires against me
White powder blows the room
An alien fills the mirror
No landing on the Moon

UFO's now cloud the skies
Led Zeppelin's had its day
Track me down the airwaves
To media gods we pray

Single shot that rocked the world
Dead presidents elect
Fat fingers press the button
We serve but not protect

Seeds that Sow

Tell me what you see
In poppy seeded flowers
An ocean full of crimson
Cast from ivory towers

Tell me what you feel
As the carpet now runs red
Do you turn from twisted faces
To dance with grateful dead

Tell me why you care
Now the last post has been sung
Across the poppy fields a blowing
Cry out ghosts of young

The Soldier

Pulling up a sandbag
Swinging on his lamp
His height I stood in wonder
My neck it got a cramp

Intent upon his gravelled voice
A thousand ciggies rolled
My heart was all a' thumping
If I should be so bold

But never was he boastful
He spoke of comrades dear
His chest all glinting medals
And a single, frozen tear

To see or purchase other books by Colin Dennis
please visit the author's website.

www.colindennisbooks.com

Printed in Great Britain
by Amazon

00029